# ESTEBAN

### A NOVEL BY
## GILBERTO FLORES PATIÑO

### TRANSLATED BY
## LINDA GABORIAU

**CORMORANT BOOKS**

The translation assistance of the Ontario Arts Council is
gratefully acknowledged.

The publisher wishes to acknowledge the assistance of the
Canada Council, the Ontario Arts Council, the Department
of Heritage, and the Government of Ontario through the
Ministry of Culture, Tourism and Recreation.

First published in Spanish by Editorial Universo in Mexico in
1985. Published in French by Les Éditions du Boréal Express in
Canada in 1987.

Edited by Gena K. Gorrell.

Front cover design by Thom Pritchard at Artcetera Graphics.
Cover illustration by Paul Perras, from the cover illustration
by Pol Turgeon for the French edition.

Printed and bound in Canada.

Published by
Cormorant Books Inc.
RR 1, Dunvegan, Ontario
Canada K0C 1J0.

Canadian Cataloguing in Publication Data

Flores Patiño, Gilberto, 1941-
[Esteban el centauro. English]
    Esteban: a novel

Translation of: Esteban el centauro.
ISBN 0-920953-92-1

    I. Title. II. Title: Esteban el centauro. English.

PS8561.L667E8813 1995    jC843'.54    C95-900649-4
PR9199.3.F56E8813 1995

*To my daughter Jenny,*
*to my son David*

# CHAPTER ONE

ESTEBAN

June 1968
When I told Señora Lena that sometimes I get tired of repeating in my head without wanting to, all the details of everything I see, everything that happens to me, she assured me that some day I'll stop doing it, that's just how it is at my age, since I'm a child I have to fill myself with memories. Later we don't notice things so much, she said, we prefer to think about how things used to be. I asked her if the tin roosters when she was young looked like the ones I see in her store and she said no, the ones she saw as a child were bigger and they played with her. Now I have to sell them, she said, they're not the same any more, they've stopped being little roosters, now they're merchandise. When they were merchandise for my father, she told

me, I got really upset when people took them away. I asked her if they played with her now and she said no, tin roosters don't play with old people, even if old people try and try to get them to. That made me sad, because some day I'm going to be old and my little horse won't play with me any more. But I know one thing, he'll never be merchandise, the two of us will always be together, because I don't have a handicrafts store like Señora Lena.

We've been together a long time. My mama bought him for me the day a lady gave me a shot because the doctor said it was the only way I'd get better. I had something that felt like a piece of meat, a huge piece, stuck in my throat, and it really hurt and my temperature wouldn't go away. I couldn't stop crying after the lady gave me the shot, no matter how hard I tried, and my mama promised to buy me a little present if I stopped. I finally calmed down, I don't know if it stopped hurting or if it was because of the present, I don't know, but she thought it was because of the present so that afternoon she brought me my little horse.

Señora Lena's right about one thing, I saw that for myself. As soon as I got home, right away, right away, I came into my room and I looked at him very carefully, more carefully than back in her store when she was telling me. Yes, Señora Lena's right, things change. Because when my mama gave him to me my little horse was bigger, or I was smaller, but that doesn't matter. Things do change. I just hope my little horse doesn't change so much that I stop noticing him, because I don't want him to turn into a wooden memory some day.

Tomorrow we'll go to the country, you and me. Do you want to go back to the same place as last Saturday? We could watch them jump over the tires, the bars and all that again.

I remember the first time I ever saw horses jump, but they were different horses, not the ones that jump on Saturdays. It was at Marcela's house. The men with their black caps, like baseball players, but with jackets and ties too. Marcela's papa said they weren't baseball caps, they were helmets to protect their heads if they fell off their horses. You saw them too, because right away you started jumping over the armchairs, the table, the chairs, the doll Marcela had left lying on the rug. Do you remember the horse that couldn't jump over some of the bars? It tripped and the man fell on the ground and hit his chest really hard. What a fall, yelled someone who sounded really frightened, but we couldn't see him because they didn't show him to us. Then the man stood up and he was clutching his chest, looking up and making faces because it hurt so much, and another man put his arm over his shoulders and they walked off, or at least we couldn't see them any more, but we could see the horse that couldn't stand up, it kept stretching its neck and struggling and kicking and kicking but it couldn't do anything. Then Marcela's papa said maybe it broke a leg. She asked him what the man would do if that's what happened to his horse and just as you were about to jump over his right foot you stopped to listen to his answer, and he said they'd shoot it. But he didn't exactly answer Marcela's question, and she didn't notice, or if she noticed she didn't know what to say or didn't want to say anything, because she'd asked him what the man would do if his horse had a broken leg and he'd told her what other people would do, they'd kill the horse. I thought the man would be really sad, you know? If something like that happened to you, I think I'd die with you. But nothing like that happened, the horse finally stood up and another man walked it off the television and took it away, but we don't know where because they didn't show us. Then other horses went on jumping, and you jumped over the shoe really well and I got scared when I saw you running towards the sofa where Marcela and her mama were sitting, because the sofa is so big and they were on it too, and I told you not to try it, that it was dangerous and you could break a leg and now you know what happens if you do, but you kept on running with my hand on your rump and I kept saying, careful, careful, but since you wouldn't stop I decided to leave you alone so you could concentrate on the jump, and when you got really close to the sofa I thought you were going to stop, not out of fear but because Marcela's papa was looking at me bent over with my feet running, as if the noise of your hoofs was bothering him, but you didn't stop, you were looking at the sofa and Marcela's head and her mama's head and you were measuring. Then you jumped slowly, flying in slow motion, as if the air had suddenly turned into water. When you were flying over Marcela's head and then over her mama's, my hand felt the same as that time I jumped off the bridge, except it's not a bridge, it's a canal that doesn't have any water now. Remember? I was holding you in my hand, but I don't know what you felt. For me it felt like fear and happiness together, like both things tumbling around in your stomach and sometimes you like the feeling and sometimes you don't and you want to throw up, and I kept on falling and falling and it seemed like the ground wasn't there any more, or someone kept moving it farther away so I'd never touch it again. That's what was happening to my hand, that's what it felt. And as soon as you started heading down towards the rug I said, careful, little horse, don't break a leg. But you didn't listen to me, you just went on flying very slowly and then you proved how strong you are, because you landed on your feet, straight up, and nothing happened to you. Then Marcela's papa told me you were a good horse and you could compete for sure with any of the horses jumping on television, but I should let you rest a bit, because he thought I was the one making you jump, but I wasn't. Anyway I told you, take a rest, little horse, and you lay there very quietly between my legs and I felt really proud you were mine and really happy you could do more things than the horses on Marcela's television. Maybe that's because you're a little bit bigger. You're twice the size of my hand, and when they run and jump they're exactly the size of my hand, no more. But that doesn't matter. Even if they were as big as the ones we see jumping in the country, they couldn't do what you do. All they do is jump on television. And you know Don Celso, the milkman, well, his horse is much, much bigger and all it does is carry Don Celso and his milk cans. Don Celso said so himself.

You know what? I'm glad it's Friday night. Tomorrow is Saturday, there's no school and we can go to the country. I'd sure be a lot happier if my mama was here with me, like Marcela's mama who comes and tells her stories at night before she falls asleep, and then gives her a kiss and tucks in her blankets. She tucks me in too, and sometimes she pats me on the head and runs her hand over your rump and says goodnight to you, when Marcela invites me to spend Friday night at her house. Maybe she would have invited me today, but she's not here, she and her papa and her mama went to another city, I can't remember its name. But my mama isn't like that, she's different. She reads me stories I don't really understand. Marcela's papa comes to give her a goodnight kiss too. He doesn't tell her stories, he just asks her if she brushed her teeth and sits for a while on the edge of her bed, then gives her a kiss and leaves. One night Marcela said to him, papa, tell me about when you were a little boy, the way you did that other time, but he said, some other day, some other day, and walked out smiling. He smiles a lot, it seems like he never gets mad, I've never seen him get mad, even when Marcela gets into mischief. Like that day we decided to make a chocolate cake in the kitchen, and we left the table covered with mud and we made such a mess in the oven! Marcela's mama got mad and she was going to spank her, but her papa came when he heard all the yelling and told her, calm down, woman, calm down, smiling as if nothing had happened, and it's true that nothing had happened, but Marcela's mama thought something awful had happened, calm down, what's the fuss, we'll clean the stove, period, they're children, he said, they're children and they don't know what they're doing. Yes they do, they do know, Marcela's mama kept yelling, really mad, not because she's mean but what we did seemed really bad to her, and when someone thinks something's bad, then it's bad, and they get mad. Yes they do, they do know, she kept saying, but we didn't know, because our chocolate cake didn't come out like Amalita's, Marcela's maid, all moist and sweet. Ours was very hard and didn't taste good, even though we let it cook in the oven for a long time. I told Marcela, no, Marcela, Amalita makes it with flour and she adds eggs and chocolate, we're doing it wrong, and she told me to be quiet, you don't know anything about cooking, she said, so I didn't say a thing, but I knew we were doing it wrong. Still, Marcela's mama wasn't right, her papa was, because Marcela didn't know what she was doing, and I saw the green cans and I knew which one had the flour, and I knew they kept the eggs in the refrigerator and the chocolate in one of the drawers, but I still wouldn't have known how to make a cake like the ones Amalita makes, so that's why Marcela's papa was right, we didn't know.

And that's when Marcela's mama told her she got into too much mischief, and it was the first time I'd heard that word in Spanish, because my mama speaks to me in English, which is why I don't always understand the stories she reads me. I speak Spanish, and everything I think, I think in Spanish. I wasn't born here, I was born in the United States, but I came here when I was so little I feel like a Mexican, not a gringo, that's why I like Spanish better.

Marcela's papa calls me Esteban the Centaur. The first time he called me this, one Friday night, I asked him what it meant, and he told me that a long long time ago there were men who had half their body like a horse, and the other half like a man, but he was saying that because of you, you know, because we're always together.

When he told me that, I looked at my body, even though I knew it hadn't changed. What if other people suddenly saw me like that? What if I only think I carry you around in my hand, and it's not true? What if you and I were one? Or what if, the night Marcela's papa said that to me, I'd really turned into a centaur? Can you imagine? We would have come home and what a shock for my mama, for mama and one of them. What a headache for my mama, worse than ever. Because she always has a headache on Saturdays, that's what she tells me when we're alone and when I don't spend the night at Marcela's, because when I do I spend the whole day there and you and I don't come home till afternoon, and my mama's head doesn't ache in the afternoon. What a headache, she says, as if she's talking to herself, as if I'm not there, or she says it to one of them and tells him to leave, they'll see each other later that afternoon or that night, because she doesn't feel well.

Once my mama was sleeping and one of them was sleeping in her bed too, and I didn't make any noise so I wouldn't wake her up, because if I wake her up she gets mad and I don't want my mama to get mad, she works so hard all week at the Institute giving her painting classes, and when I make noise on Saturday mornings and wake her up and she gets mad, she tells me she has the right to have fun and the right to sleep and get some rest, because she works so hard all week, but I think, even though she's saying all that to me, she's not talking to me but to someone else, someone she's really mad at, madder than she is at me for waking her up without meaning to, because her face gets red red red and she yells at me really loud, as if I was nothing to her, as if I was her worst enemy.

That time I got up very carefully, as usual, but sometimes I can't help an accident, and I tried not to make any noise, not to trip over the cans of paint or the other things she uses for her work and leaves on the floor all over the house, and I saw them sleeping and even though I didn't go near them, and I could smell paint and turpentine, I was sure my mama's mouth smelled the way it smells on Saturdays. Then I went into the kitchen and took out the cereal and the milk and fixed my breakfast, and I was watching you standing there quietly beside my bowl, looking as if you were hungry, as if you felt like tasting my breakfast, when he came in. He had gotten up, but not my mama.

From the table, I could see her asleep in her bed.

His eyes were really red and they kept closing, as if he wanted to wake up but his eyes didn't, and he put his hand on the back of his neck and turned his head from side to side, then up and down, as if it really hurt and he wanted to get rid of the pain that way. You can't get rid of the pain that way, I know that, so I told him my mother had some aspirin in the bathroom. But he told me he wanted a cup of coffee, and I went to get the jar for him, because he didn't know where my mama keeps it and he couldn't find it. Then he put the water on the stove and made himself a cup of coffee.

He came and sat beside us, remember? And there we were, me eating my cereal and him drinking his coffee, as if we were having breakfast together.

What's your name?, he asked me, and I told him Esteban, and I would have liked to add the centaur, when he started staring at you with his red eyes, but I didn't, I didn't have time because he asked me, do you like horses? and I told him, my little horse, you, yes. A little wooden horse, he said and he patted you. His hand was really shaking and I saw him get sad and I thought he was thinking of his own horse, and I asked him, do you have one? He said no, with his head, but I could see how sad he was so I asked him if he had one when he was a little boy and lost it so he didn't have it any more, and he told me no, it was his son who had one.

When I asked him where his son lived, he said Troy, then he said, the Trojan horse, and I didn't know if Troy was the name of the city where his son lived, or his son's name, even if Troy didn't seem like a boy's name to me, but there are lots of things I don't know so I asked him, what does that mean?

And I remember that he put his arm on the table and then his chin on his arm and went on staring at you. And then he told me the story of a city called Troy, and how one day there was a war and the enemies of the city built a wooden horse, a very very very big one, and how they hid in the belly of the horse, right here, he said, and he touched your stomach with the tip of his finger, and how they left the horse at the gate of the city and the men of Troy brought it inside, because the city had walls all around it and the enemies couldn't get in because the people of Troy defended themselves really well, and how this was the only way they were able to get in, and how, once they were inside, they opened the horse's stomach, right here, he said, and he poked you with his finger again, and they came out, he said, and they began to fight and they beat the people of Troy.

And your son has this horse, I asked him, and he smiled, really sad you know, and he messed up my hair and said no, my son's horse is a rocking-horse. And I thought about a boy rocking on his horse and about lots of enemies sliding off while he rocked, like little plastic soldiers coming out of holes in the stomach of a wooden horse, and I imagined a battle around his son's feet, on the floor of his room.

Then he got up and went to get dressed, because when he was drinking his coffee he was only wearing his undershirt and underpants. After he finished dressing he came to the door of the kitchen and said, goodbye Esteban, and I said goodbye to him, and he left. I never saw him again and I never asked my mama about him, because once I asked her who they were and she told me never to ask her that.

Now we have to sleep, because tomorrow we're going to the country to watch the horses jump.

# CHAPTER TWO

ESTEBAN

I can tell we're not going to meet anyone today. My mama wasn't in the house when we left, she hadn't come home yet. Her bed was still made, just like last night. I ate my cereal very slowly in case she got back before we left, but she didn't. I didn't want to wait any longer because I'd told you we were coming here. But the horses aren't here today either. What should we do? Do you feel like going to Marcela's house? Me too, but I don't think she's back yet, well, I really don't know. I guess we should just stay here a bit longer, and give her time to come back, in case she's still in that other city. Listen, why don't you jump? You can do it as well as the other horses. Go ahead, take my hand for a ride, start jumping. Let's see, let's see, let's see, which one do you want, where do you want to begin? But

— 21 —

you have to jump over all of them. Even that really tall one that looks like a brick wall. We're going to jump over these two first, and then the tallest one, the one that looks like a wall, all right? That's the way, little horse, that's the way. Run. Giddyup, giddyup, giddyup, that's the way. Ah, you feel good when you're running in the country, don't you? Okay, I won't distract you, think about the jump, think about those tires sticking halfway out of the ground. Let's go, start running with my hand on your rump. Giddyup, giddyup, giddyup. Jump! Good boy, good boy, what a good jump! It wasn't too high, was it? Yes, it was very high, but you're a very strong little horse and you can really jump. Now you have to run to those bars and jump over them without making a single one fall, without even hitting them with your hoofs, okay? Let's go! Giddyup giddyup giddyup. Jump! Good. Oooff! You almost couldn't do it. Because my arm isn't that long. But you jumped, you really did jump. Now that one, the one that looks like a brick wall. Let's go! Giddyup giddyup giddyup. Oh, too bad, little horse, I can't reach it, my arm isn't long enough yet, I'm just a little boy. How can we do it? Maybe if I climb up here.

*

I'm really sorry, little horse, you still felt like jumping over the one like a brick wall. Look, from here I can see the man who told me, don't climb up there, boy, because you could knock over the obstacle and I don't feel like setting it up again. But I didn't answer him and I didn't get down for a long time, because you were concentrating hard on the jump and I was so surprised by his voice that I stayed still as if I couldn't move, so he asked me if I was a little gringo who didn't understand Spanish. Then I climbed down, and once I was on the ground I told him, I'm a Mexican. Ah, he said, then how come you're so fair? I'm a Mexican, just like you. No, boy, not like me, look, I'm very dark, and he raised his sombrero a bit, as if I hadn't been able to see his face. His hair was really short, like Don Celso's, and he was dressed the same way. My mama says that people who dress like Don Celso are campesinos, and that campesinos work in the fields sowing corn and beans. And I asked him if he sowed corn and beans and he told me he used to, but now he was working with Señor Black and he was in charge of his horses and the obstacles, and I stood there and looked around at the bars and the tires stuck in the ground, and at the one that looks like a brick wall and all the others.

That's when the man noticed you and said, don't tell me your little horse jumps over obstacles, and I said yes you do, and he smiled. Then he asked me if you ran really fast and I said yes again. Do you think he runs faster than the ones that will be here soon?, he asked me, and I said yes, faster than them. That's when you started to run, giddyup, giddyup, giddyup, and you stopped here under this tree, because you were looking at the grass and you hadn't eaten breakfast yet.

That's where Don Celso lives, over there. I don't

know where, but it's over there. Once I asked him where
he brought his milk from and he said, from the barn,
and I asked him where his barn was and he said, next
to his house, and I asked where his house was and he
said it was in the country, beyond El Atascadero,
Esteban, he said. El Atascadero is where those houses
are. One of those houses is Marcela's.

So it's over there. But where? From here we can only
see the white white earth and the grass and the trees
and the little trees, because the farther away they are,
the smaller they are.

Who knows which way Don Celso goes to get to
his house? Really close to here there's a road, but there's
another one over there. And then there's the paved one
that leads to the highway beyond that stone arch across
from the gas station.

The country is really big and you can go lots of
places if you set out without knowing and start
travelling around, but only Don Celso knows how to
get to his house, well, him and the people who know
him and the people who know him and know the
country, because I know him but I don't know all the
country, only a tiny bit.

Two dirt roads, little horse. Where do the dirt roads
go? They come from over there, look, as if they came
out of El Atascadero. Only they don't come out of there,
it's just that the paved streets end and the people and
the cars can't stop, because when someone's on the road
it's because he's going somewhere, and he can't stop
until he reaches where he's going, and if the road stops

he makes his own road. Where do these roads go, little horse? It's no secret, they go to the farms. Way, way, way over there, very far away, is where the farms are. Don Celso lives over there.

Do you see how the roads are? Well, right now you can't see anything because you're eating your breakfast. But you've seen them before. It looks like a very very very big boy walked through here and made the roads with two fingers. Because look, every one of them has sort of two little canals separated by earth that the boy's fingers didn't move. When he passed through here both his hands were busy, for sure.

Where does the boy who makes roads walk now? Eh, can you imagine, there are so many roads like this in the country, many many many, as soon as you leave one of the paved streets, right away you see one of those little roads, well, not always, because that highway begins where one of the paved streets ends, but almost all of them end with roads like this. They're all over the place. Can you imagine that boy sitting against a tree like me, trying to count all the roads he's made?

I'm going to make a little road here, look, to join this tree trunk to another one and then another one. Three little roads. Oh, look how it came out, little horse. It looks like my grandma's shop in the United States. I don't know if you remember it, because we were there a long time ago, last year. Señora Lena says last year isn't very long ago at all, that's just the way we see things when we're young and time seems to stretch out and the days seem to drag on and on and on, as if they were never going to end. But when we grow up time goes by like water, and last year seems like yesterday. That's what Señora Lena said, time goes by like water. And she also says she never sees the day go by. That means it doesn't seem long to her and she never has time to do everything she has to do, because she says no sooner does the sun rise than it's night again, before you know it. That's what she says.

That's how it is for me on Saturday and Sunday. I don't see time go by, it goes by like water. Because the days we have school seem very long to me. And that's not because I don't like school, I do. I'm with other children there, some of them are my friends, like Marcela and Roberto, others are kids I know. What happens is, there are things I don't like, like math. I don't like math at all. I like grammar, well, I don't like the verbs, or I like them but not a lot, even if I don't find them so hard.

What I really like is when Señorita Estela tells us what every word means. And once I started to wonder, who could have invented words? Every word, little horse, can you imagine? Once I asked Señorita Estela, isn't it true that the lady who invented words wrote them down in the dictionary so they wouldn't be forgotten? And she asked me why I thought it was a lady and I told her, because ladies are the ones who know more than everyone, and she asked me why I believed that and I told her, because I had three other lady teachers before her so ladies are the ones who know more, and she said, but there are men teachers too, and I said yes, there are men teachers too, but I never had one and I don't know if they know as many things as the ladies. Then she came over to my seat and gave me a kiss and told me that people invented words together. Well, she didn't really say that just to me but to everyone, because we were all in the classroom.

She said that many years ago people didn't know how to talk, they only made sort of grunting noises with their mouths, but one day a miracle happened. That's what she said, a miracle. Somebody, a man or a woman, or an old person, was able to give a name to something, he or she said stone, tree, animal, and then repeated that first word, again and again and again. And then all his friends started to say that word and point to the same thing, and they all agreed that was what they'd call that thing. But there were many more things, many many more, said Señorita Estela, so then someone else gave a name to something else, and some other person said the word sky and another one said the word road and so on.

That's what she said, and then I asked her, isn't it true that one of those people decided to write the new word in the dictionary right away so that if someone forgot it he'd know where to find it?

And Señorita Estela smiled and said no, it was a long time before someone invented writing. Then she said something I really liked, she said the first notebook men had was their memory and the first pencil was their eyes. And I told her no, well, I didn't say no, I said their pencil had five points, and she asked me why I said that and I told her, because they wrote in their memory what they saw, what they smelled, what they heard, what they felt and the taste of things, and everyone in the classroom laughed and she stared at me in a way that scared me, because she stopped smiling and wrinkled her forehead and I thought, she thinks I was wrong to say the pencil had more than one point, which is what she said, and I was sure there was nothing wrong with that, but I know when someone thinks something is wrong, for that person it is wrong, and then the person gets mad, but the teacher didn't get mad, instead she came back and gave me another kiss and this time she gave me a big hug and told me, you're right, Esteban, you're right.

I have a dictionary at home. Well, there are three dictionaries in my house. One in English, only English. Another half in English and half in Spanish. Those two are my mama's. Even though I read them sometimes too, when I need to know what a word means in English. My poor mama doesn't speak Spanish very well, and she gets very frustrated when she goes to buy something in the market or when she talks with one of those men who doesn't speak English. But I'm sure she's going to learn, it's just that she needs to talk more and she doesn't talk much because she paints and she gets all quiet when she paints. She loves to paint. She told me that's why she stopped taking Spanish classes, because it takes too much time. I try to help her at home and I tell her how you say this or that, but she gets frustrated and tells me she's never going to be able to speak Spanish. I know she will, because now she knows more words than before, she just doesn't realize it.

The other one is mine. It's a small dictionary, very very very small. It doesn't have many words. Much much less than my mama's dictionaries. I didn't count them but you can see it right away. It has only a few words, as if they'd been written there by a child who doesn't know a lot of words yet. But of course that child knows more words than me, because there are lots of words I don't know, but some day I'm going to know them. How will I learn? I have to read my dictionary over and over. But no matter how much I read it and read it, I still forget a lot of them, because I don't say them.

But that's because there are words nobody says, not even Señora Lena or Don Celso, or Marcela or her mama and papa, or Roberto or the others, or Señorita Estela or Señora Green, but they are written in books. So I have to read a lot, so the books can say them to me and I won't forget them.

Look, little horse, let's pretend these are the roads to my grandma's shop. Do you remember what it's like there?

There are three roads, but they're not dirt roads, they're more like the highway that goes by the gas station, over there near the arch. And they're really wide highways, well, two of them are, not the other one, the other one is narrower. That's the one that leads to the shop and the gasoline pump, because my grandma sells gasoline too. You know, she sells lots of things in the shop. Cookies and chips and candies and little bags of peanuts and beer and pop and bottles of wine, lots of things. She even sells charcoal in thick paper bags. Because over there people sometimes cook outside in the yard, in the yard of their house, so they buy charcoal and burn it and cook the chicken or steaks or whatever they're going to eat and they put a red sauce on the chicken, and they call that barbecued chicken, I saw all that in the house of one of my mama's friends. I tried the red sauce, it doesn't burn like chile, but I like chile sauce better even though my mama doesn't like it and that's why she never makes it. Anyway she doesn't have time to cook, that's why at home we always eat bread and ham and mayonnaise and mustard and peanut butter and jam and cereal and milk and soup in cans. But sometimes she takes me to eat in a restaurant and then I eat chile, even though my mama tells me she doesn't know how I can like something so hot, and I tell her I like it because that's what we all like, all us Mexicans, and she laughs. And I tell her to taste it and she'll see that it's good and it's not too hot, just spicy. But she won't taste it and she tells me, I don't even want to touch it.

Sometimes people stare at us in the restaurant and they must wonder how we understand each other, because she speaks to me in English and I always speak Spanish, except when she doesn't understand I say it in English so she'll understand. But I don't really like talking like this. That's why I prefer Señorita Estela's classes, but not because Señora Green is grouchy or anything like that, no, she's very nice. At first I thought she was grouchy, because she's the principal and she's always very serious in her office, but whenever she spends time with us and starts teaching us the things she knows and explaining things in the books that we don't understand, we realize that she's very nice and she has a very soft voice and she never gets mad. But it has nothing to do with her, it's just that I like Spanish better. And I like Señorita Estela better too, I don't know why, but I like her better.

Anyway, this is my grandma's shop, here in the tree, okay? If I had a little jack-knife I'd carve the door and the windows. But it's a good thing I don't have one, because it would hurt the tree. Did you know that trees feel it when someone carves them with a knife? I didn't know that. People think that we're the only ones who have feelings, us persons, and that we feel everything. Then we think that animals have feelings, but that they feel less than us, and that's not so sure, little horse. My mother told me that trees and animals feel things just like us.

Can you imagine how much it hurt the tree you came from when they were making you?

Except that's not how it was. First the woodcutters knocked down the tree, then they divided it into pieces and by then the tree didn't feel anything any more. Later someone saw you sort of hidden in one of the pieces of the tree. He was the only one who could see you, no one else. And he started to clean your rump and your legs, your head and your tail. Bit by bit he removed all the wood that was hiding you, until you came out the way you are now, and you came galloping galloping galloping from the woods to the shop where my mama bought you for me.

Who could your papa be, little horse? Who made you? Your mama was the wood of the tree. But who was your papa? And who was mine?

You don't know, and I don't either. My mama's never told me. Once I asked her and she told me that he lives in the United States. But she doesn't have a picture or anything and I don't know what his face looks like. And when I asked her his name she said she'd forgotten it, but I'm not sure that's true, it's just because she doesn't want to tell me.

And I asked her if he's a painter like her and she went like this, humpf!, and she said no, he works in a bank, he'd rather make money.

And I thought about a man with a machine with a handle and a spout, and I could see him turning the handle, making lots of money pour out the spout of the machine. But I couldn't see his face because I've never seen it. All I could see was his body and sort of a cloud of smoke around his shoulders.

Then I asked her why he doesn't live with us, and she said no, he doesn't live with us, that's how it is. But I already knew that and that wasn't what I was asking. So I asked her again and she told me that later on she'd tell me, that for now there are a lot of things I can't understand.

So, little horse, guess I have to wait, right?, to find out why my papa doesn't live with us.

But anyway, let's say that we'd go from San Miguel de Allende to see my grandma along this road. It's a very long trip, little horse, I don't know if you remember. We spent days and days, the three of us, in the bus. Now try to imagine that trip on horseback. You'd be really tired. Just think, you wouldn't be carrying only me, because we're not going to leave my mama here, right?

So then we'd get there tired and covered with dust, and very hungry, little horse. And my grandma would come out to meet us and she'd hug me and give me a kiss. I can even feel her body, chubby chubby chubby. Because she's really chubby. Do you remember what she's like? And inside the shop those same men would be having a beer and they'd say hello to me and I'd say hello to them, and then since I'd be really hungry I'd start eating chips and candy and I'd open a bottle of orange pop, the kind I like so much but my mama won't let me have because she says it ruins my teeth. But this time she wouldn't say no and I'd drink it all every drop of it. Then since you'd be hungry too we'd go out into the fields, to that place where the grass grows so tall and green, where those cows and horses were, remember? Where the men were gathering up the grass in sort of blocks that come out of a machine, near those apple trees. And I'd give you an apple and you'd eat it. I can even hear you chewing on it, little horse.

Then at night we'd watch my grandma's colour TV. I love to watch television even if we don't have one because my mama says she doesn't like it because there's too much violence. But I watch it at Marcela's house or Roberto's, but more at Marcela's because I hardly ever go to Roberto's. And we'd watch the girls who live with their papa and their mama in the prairie.

The prairie is a field, little horse, and it has very green grass. Here the countryside is different but I like it a lot, even though it doesn't have as much grass and there aren't a lot of trees like where my grandma lives, where it looks a lot like the prairie they show on television. I like it a lot because it's the country of the city where we live, you and me and my mama. And I like this city a lot because it's my city, even though I wasn't born here. I can't imagine leaving this city ever, little horse. We're always going to live here, you and my mama and me. And some day I'm going to be big and my mama won't have to work so hard at the Institute and she'll be able to rest as much as she wants, because I'm going to work for her and you'll always be with me and we'll go to work together.

What kind of work would I like to do?

Roberto says he's going to be an astronaut when he's big and he brings books to school that have photographs of space and the spaceships.

I like looking at those books, with all the colours in the sky. Even though all we can see is the little white dots of the stars at night, and in daytime we can only see the sky all blue like right now, or sometimes there are clouds but no rain, behind all that there are lots of colours.

The planet I like best is Saturn, with its rings, and

that other one, the sort of dark cloud that looks like you, far far away.

I didn't know there are noises in the sky that nobody can hear, but there are, Roberto says so. And he shows us photographs of things like plates that must be very big, and he says they're machines that can hear the noise the stars make.

He says the men working on this have discovered stars by the noise they make, before they saw them shining in the sky. It's as if they follow their noise until they finally catch up with them.

Marcela says when she's big she's going to be a doctor, a specialist, and she'll always get up when people call her in the middle of the night to treat a sick person and she won't charge much money. Because she says Amalita's sister was very sick one night and no doctor wanted to get up to go treat her and afterwards she got sicker and they had to take her to the hospital the next day, but she died there because they couldn't take her to the specialist, and she says Amalita was crying really hard when she asked Marcela's papa where they could have found the money to take her to a specialist because those doctors charge so much and that's why she died.

But I don't want to be an astronaut like Roberto, and not because I don't like the photographs in his books but because, I don't know why, but I just don't feel like being an astronaut. And I don't want to be a specialist and charge very little like Marcela either, and not because I want poor people to be sick and to be

taken to the hospital and then die, no, but just because
this isn't what I want to be when I'm big.

Once I told Roberto what I'd like to be and he
laughed and he said, you're crazy, what's the point of
collecting a bunch of words and writing them down in
a dictionary?

But that's what I want to be, I said, and he told me
again that I'm crazy. That's what I'm going to do
anyway, I told him.

Then Roberto said it wasn't a job and I told him it
was, and he said okay, maybe it is a job, but I wouldn't
want to spend my life at a printer's lining up little letters
to make words and then making them come out on a
piece of paper, don't tell me you'd like doing that, he
said.

I remembered the men who were doing that at the
printer's Señora Green took us to visit once, and I told
him that's not what I meant and I told him again and
he didn't understand, and then I had to explain to him
that yes, the books he brings to school are made at a
printer's, but first there was a man who found the
photographs and the words, and then he told the people
at the printer's what to do with all that, and finally
Roberto understood.

But he told me he thought it would be more
interesting to be an astronaut anyway, and that's what
he was going to be when he was big. Well, good for
him, right?

There's something else I'd like to do too, little horse.
Have you ever noticed Marcela's papa's books?

They look a bit like the ones my mama has. Well, they're books too, but they're really beat up and one of them doesn't even have a cover. There are about five of them beside the dictionaries, that's all, and they're not like my school books either. No, I mean like Marcela's father's books. I'd like to make a book like those books. But you need paper for the pages and leather for the covers and I don't have any of that.

I write things in my school notebook, even though it belongs to the school that's where I write. But not very much, because I don't know what to write about. All I can do is start by saying that I have a little wooden horse who goes everywhere with me, and that my mama loves to paint and that Señora Lena has a handicrafts shop where she sells tin roosters and mirrors and lots of other things and that Marcela lives in El Atascadero and that Roberto wants to be an astronaut and that Don Celso has a horse he delivers the milk with, and I also write about my school and about Señora Green and Señorita Estela. And it's always the same thing. I don't have much to write about.

Then I think about what Señora Lena says, that I'm a child filling himself with memories. So I guess I'll have to wait a while to have something to remember and to write, and then buy the paper for the books and take everything to the printer's so they can make me a book like the ones I'm telling you about. But will they put the leather on the covers at the printer's too? Well, I'll find out where later.

But these are the two things I like, and that's what

I'm going to do when I grow up. I hope I'll be able to earn enough money doing that so my mama won't have to work so hard at the Institute and I'll be able to spend more time with her.

Let's go now, little horse, let's go see if Marcela is back. I'd like to go see my mama, but she must be sleeping and I don't want to wake her up and make her mad at me. I'll see her later this afternoon.

*

From up here on these rocks we can see the dam and the whole lake, little horse. Marcela can't see it with us because she still isn't back from the city where she went with her papa and her mama. And Amalita said she didn't know what time they'd be back.

This dam isn't like the big one. That one's almost like the sea. They say it goes all the way to Dolores Hidalgo. Do you remember we went there once? Señora Green took us there so we could see one of those factories where they make pretty tiles and dishes, over there in Dolores.

We went to two factories. The one in Dolores Hidalgo where there are ovens to make things out of clay. And when we were there Marcela and I remembered our chocolate cake and that made us laugh, and the others asked us why we were laughing but we didn't tell them.

And we also went to that other one farther down the road, where they make muslin and I guess other cloth but I can't remember. Uh, there are lots of machines that make a lot of noise, really loud noise. And we all covered our ears so they wouldn't explode. And there were men taking care of the machines without covering their ears, and they were even laughing. I don't think I could stay there very long, well, maybe I could after my ears exploded. Then so what? I wouldn't be able to hear the noise. And I could stay there and take care of the machines.

There was lots of dust in the air too, and the man who was showing us around the factory was saying something to us so we unblocked our ears and he yelled really loud but it sounded quiet to us, and he told us how that fuzz is very bad for the lungs and that's why the workers have to wear little masks so they don't breathe it in. But the men were wearing the masks around their necks, as if they were breathing through their throats.

This dam isn't the big one. But for you and for me it seems very big. I'd like to cross the water in a boat. Well, in a little boat made of paper. But we'd have to be really tiny. Otherwise our boat would sink. Then this lake would seem as big as the other one, the one that's almost like the sea. Well, not really the same, I say that but it's not true. Because the sea is really big, really really big. Huge! It holds a lot a lot of water.

I've only seen the sea once. That was when my mama took me to a place called Puerto Angel. I was much smaller than now, and you hadn't come to live with me yet. I don't remember very much. But I remember my mama put my bathing suit on me and I played with my pail and my shovel and I made little piles of sand and the sea would come and unmake them. And I remember one man brought a dog with him and the dog ran along the beach behind the man, because the man was running too.

My mama and her friends would go walking looking at the sand and picking up shells and one lady held one to her ear and laughed and said she could hear the sea. So I thought the sea was talking and its voice came out of shells, because all the men and women and my mama put shells to their ears and started laughing and saying yes yes, I can hear it too. And since no one said what the sea was saying, I found a shell and stuck it to my ear, but I couldn't hear a thing, and since they kept saying they heard it I thought my shell wasn't any good and I threw it away and found another one and I still couldn't hear anything, and I went on looking and looking but I couldn't hear the voice of the sea in any of the shells. Then I went over to my mama and I took her shell and held it to my ear just like her, but I still couldn't hear anything. So I thought only big people can hear the sea when it speaks through shells.

Sometimes I stick one of the shells we have at home to my ear and I tell my mama I'm going to hear the sea and she says, that's good. But I only say that, because I can't hear anything. Do you hear it? I ask her and she says yes. What's the sea saying?, I ask her and she says I have to listen very hard and I'll discover it myself, but I can't hear anything no matter how long I hold the shell to my ear.

Guess I have to wait till I'm big to listen to the words of the sea. So you see, little horse, I realize children always have to wait.

I can hardly remember the noise the sea made. It's like the wind. Yes, little horse, it's like the wind and lots of leaves. You don't understand? Well, then it's like the wind passing through the trees. That's all I can tell you, because that's what I remember. But I'm not sure about that, maybe I imagine it that way because I've already forgotten.

If you and I made ourselves tiny tiny, so tiny we could fit into a paper boat to sail across that lake, we'd listen to the sound of the wind in the trees and we'd think we were on the sea.

Can you imagine how big the trees would look? Huge trees! And the grass would look high too. We could go exploring in the grass, like when we walk through the reeds. And the insects would seem like monsters. And when we reached those ruins we'd think they were ruins of a destroyed city where giants lived a long long time ago. But we wouldn't walk around there at night, because at night I'd be afraid we'd end up at the ruins of the giants' destroyed city.

Our little paper boat would have to be very strong so that what happened to my grandfather wouldn't happen to us. His boat sank in the sea and he drowned and nobody ever saw him again.

That's what my grandma told me standing in front of his picture, when I asked her where he was. And later on she showed me a hat and a black overcoat that she keeps in the closet that look just like the hat and coat I saw on my grandpa in the picture. But my grandma told me sailors have more than one uniform.

That's why I never saw my grandpa. Well, I did, in his picture. But that's not the same thing.

Then I told my grandma I'd like to meet my uncle and she told me I didn't have an uncle, so I told her my aunt then and she said I didn't have an aunt either, or any cousins or anything, that I only had her and my mama, that was all, and I said my papa too and she said no. Is he dead?, I asked her and she said no and then I said, you see, you see, I have him, and again she said no, just me and your mama. And I asked her what his name was and she was about to tell me when my mama said, please don't even mention that name.

And I was really surprised, little horse, because all the boys and girls I know have uncles and aunts and cousins and their papa lives with them, unless he died, then he doesn't. Well, Glenda's papa doesn't live with her and her mama either, same thing with Peterson, and it's not just something that happens to gringos because Rosaura is Mexican and so are her mama and her papa and he doesn't live with them and he isn't dead. And there are gringos who all live together, like Fox and some others. I don't know why it's like this, but some day I'll know.

*

I love chips, I really really love them. But today I don't have any money to buy some. I think it's already time to eat because I'm beginning to feel hungry. If I could I'd go in and buy myself a bag of chips, a huge bag! Or even if it was a small one. And an orange pop too.

That shop is where Jesús lives. Once I came here and bought a bag of chips and I gave him some and the boy told me Jesús loves them, if you give them to him he'll eat them all, and he was crunching on them as if he was eating crispy meat. But I didn't give them all to him, because I love chips too. Jesús is a striped cat, half red, half yellow. But right now he's not on the counter, which is where I usually see him when I pass by here.

I think we better go home now, little horse. Then I can eat a peanut-butter and jam sandwich, but a real big one! My mama must be awake by now. Anyway I'll open the door without making a lot of noise. I'll slip the key in quiet quiet quiet, just in case she's still sleeping.

# CHAPTER THREE

ESTEBAN

W here could my mama have gone? I guess she got up and left the house already. But now it's almost night-time and she hasn't come back.

Maybe she's gone looking for me. No, I say that but I know she never goes looking for me, and when I come back and she's here, she's just here, she's not waiting for me.

Even though I'm just a little boy she says nothing bad can happen to me. I told her that Marcela's mama says that's not true. But my mama says anyway I have to learn to take care of myself. And that's what I'm doing.

And what if today is different and she went looking for me and calling me? Esteban Esteban Esteban come home.

I think I better go to the town square and see if I can find her. To tell you the truth, I want to see her.

Let's go, little horse, come with me. When I get back I'll go on reading my dictionary, because I can't read it very well right now.

I think my mama had a great idea when she told me to hang the key around my neck. Oooo, I don't know how many keys I lost before I put it on this string. Just think, without it today maybe I wouldn't have been able to get into the house.

It's going to be dark in no time. They'll turn on the lights and the streets will be different. In the daytime they're not the same as at night.

When I go by here on my way to school in the morning, everything is so bright, and even if it's a tiny bit cold I know it won't be cold later because the sun is on its way. In the afternoon the air gets colder and colder because the sun is leaving. Afterwards everything gets dark. Well, it doesn't really get dark because they turn on the lights.

I haven't seen the man who turns on the streetlights. He carries a long stick. He stops on that corner and stands there looking at the wires. Then he takes his stick and pokes around up there in the middle of the wires, who knows what he does, and the lights go on.

His name is Don Abel. I know that because once a man asked him, are you about to turn on the lights, Don Abel?, and Don Abel said, what choice do I have? And that's how I found out his name.

Once I met him myself and I said, hello Don Abel, and he said, hello child.

I hardly ever see him. Because when it starts to get dark I go home. I don't like to go walking down the streets at night. It's not because I'm afraid, little horse, because you know my mama says nothing bad can happen to me, and besides I have to learn how to take care of myself. But I like the streets better in the daytime. When it gets dark there's something different about them, something I don't like, even if I don't know what it is.

Look at the church tower, little horse. Once I bought a postcard for my grandma, well, I didn't buy it myself, I told my mama to buy it so we could show it to her the next time we went to see her. My mama told me she had already sent her one so we didn't have to buy another. Was it at night-time like this one?, I asked my mama and she said no, but that didn't matter. Then I begged her and begged her and she finally bought it.

When we were in the United States I showed it to her and I told her, it's very high, grandma, and when they light it up at night it looks like it's made of gold, look, I said.

I'd only really seen it lit up once, the time my mama took me to see the fireworks and we sat on one of these benches and she bought a bag of popcorn and we ate it.

But I couldn't see the fireworks because I was too sleepy. It was really late. I've seen them in a film that Marcela's papa shows us sometimes at her house, but that's not the same thing. All I can remember is, I heard lots of thunder that made me scared and I opened my eyes and I closed them again because the light from the fireworks hurt them. Now I ask my mama to take me again but she won't, because she says they go on late at night and I can't stay awake that late and if I fall asleep she can't carry me any more, because I'm bigger now and I weigh too much. So I stay at home and fall asleep and the thunder of the fireworks never wakes me up, maybe because my house isn't as close as the benches in the square.

But the clouds are much much much farther away, and when it rains hard and there's thunder it does wake me up. For sure, thunderstorms can be heard all over the world, well, maybe not all over the world but in all of San Miguel, because the clouds are more powerful than fireworks. And that thunder does make me scared, really scared, little horse. But we're lucky because it hardly ever rains here, so I can sleep without worrying about that.

Let's walk around the square, little horse, and see if my mama is sitting on one of the benches.

Then, you know what?, my grandma asked me, real real gold? No, grandma, I told her, it just looks like gold. That's because she's never been to San Miguel and she doesn't know how things are here.

Later on my mama told her about the bullfights, because she asked her about them. Ooof, little horse, my poor grandma, she was almost crying while my mama was describing it.

That's so cruel, so cruel, I don't want to hear any

more!, she kept saying, and then she made her stop talking and she looked mad when she said, really, Emily, I don't know how you could go there, and did you take the child with you? My mama had to tell her the truth. Poor little boy, said my grandma, and she hugged me.

That was the only time I went. I don't like going to the bullfights because they kill the bulls and when they roar it's awful. Roberto makes fun of me and says I don't go because I'm a gringo. But I tell him I'm not a gringo, I'm Mexican, so that's not why. Besides, I tell him, my mama is a gringo and she goes to the bullfights and she even did a painting with a toreador and a bull in the middle of the ring. So that's not why.

What I do like is watching the danzantes when they come to dance here in front of the parish church. My mama says they're Indians but I tell her no, they're not Indians, well, yes they're Indians, but they're called danzantes.

The next time I go to the United States I'm going to take a photograph to my grandma and I'm going to tell her what the danzantes are like. With their blue and red and green feathers and their colourful capes that spin around them and the way they play their guitars and dance and dance and dance and they never seem to get tired. I'm going to tell her how there are children danzantes too, and I wish they'd dress me up like that some day and let me dance with the boys and girls.

Ah, you know what else I'm going to take her? A record just like the one Señorita Estela played for us one day in class. That record has all the sounds of San

Miguel. The bells of the parish church, the birds that
sing here in the square and in the houses, a burro
braying and all the noises, all all all the noises we have
here. So she can imagine what it's like.

Where could my mama be? She's not on any of the
benches. Let's sit down for a while and maybe we'll see
her walk by. I really feel like seeing her. I never go out
looking for her, but today I did. Why is that, little horse?
I don't know why I feel like seeing her, well, I feel like
seeing her because she's my mama. But I never go out
looking for her. Why is that?

# CHAPTER FOUR

ESTEBAN

D id I fall asleep? What time do you think it is? I'm going to look at the alarm clock in my mama's room. You stay there all quiet and warm in my bed, next to my dictionary. Look, it's still open to the i's, right beside us.

She hasn't come back yet. The light is still on, just the way I left it. It's quarter past ten. Where could she be? It makes me feel like going to look for her. Even though she's told me never to go looking for her, because I'll get very mad, she says. But I'd just like to see her from a distance, without letting her see me.

I'll wait a little bit longer, and if she doesn't come home I'll go.

Little horse little horse, sometimes I wish I had a brother or a sister. Don't think I don't love you when I feel like this, it's not true. I love being with you and having you with me, in fact we're like brothers. No, I mean a flesh and blood brother or sister, like me, to talk to and to keep me company when my mama isn't here, like now. Of course, you and me we keep each other company. But I mean company like I am. You know what I mean.

No, little horse, you don't know what I mean and you don't listen to me. You're made of wood. I know that. I pretend to talk to you, I pretend you listen to me because you're a little toy I love very much, but you can't understand me.

I'm going to tell you something I feel, little horse. I feel afraid. My mama says it's stupid to feel afraid. Well, I feel afraid anyway, even if it's stupid.

I don't care if Roberto says only women feel afraid and that's why all the astronauts are men. I don't care because maybe it's not true. I feel afraid and I'm not a woman. I'm a little boy who will grow up and be a man later on. That's why Roberto is wrong and some day I'm going to tell him he's wrong. And if I don't feel like jumping off the wall at school into the old tires, I won't do it, and I won't care if he tells me I'm acting like a woman and I won't let that make me feel sad.

I know men can feel afraid, and I'm sure it has nothing to do with being a man or not. And if women feel afraid, well, it's because there are things that make people afraid.

Like silence.

My house is silent right now, even though I'm

talking. But it's not the same as having someone standing in front of you talking to you.

Being alone makes you afraid too.

The house is silent and I'm all alone.

Night-time makes you afraid too.

But what makes me feel most afraid? Let's see. I don't know if it's silence, because when my mama's here and I wake up because I'm thirsty or something I can hear the silence of the house, but it doesn't make me afraid, only if I had a nightmare. Then it does. But after that the fear goes away, because I know it's a nightmare, that's all.

Being alone in my house doesn't always make me feel afraid. Lots of times I stay alone, even at night. So why am I so afraid today? As if I'd had a nightmare. But even though I fell asleep I didn't have one. I can't explain it.

I'm going to read my dictionary out loud. That way it will be as if the person who gathered all the words is saying them to me, and explaining what they mean. And if I get tired of this I can write in my notebook until my mama comes home, and then we can fall asleep and I won't feel afraid any more.

Iceberg. A large floating mass of ice, detached from a glacier. There are lots of them at the North Pole, that's what they say here. Can you imagine, little horse? A mountain of ice wandering around the sea, floating like a boat. Wow, it must be cold in that boat! But you know it's not a boat, I already told you it's a huge piece of ice the size of a very very very big hill. Can you imagine how cold it is? Colder than it is here in January, much much colder.

Once Señora Green told us that, and I said nobody could live around there because sometimes when it's really cold here I don't even want to leave my house, I just want to stay inside. But she said yes, people live there and they go out all bundled up. Then Marcela asked her what they do when they're all bundled up and the sun is shining, and Señora Green said it didn't matter, the sun wasn't hot there, it looked like a bright ball way up in the sky but it didn't do any good.

She also told us there are polar bears. I know what polar bears are, I said, because once we went to Mexico City and my mama took me to the museum and then to the zoo and we saw some there.

They're white, like rabbits. But much bigger than rabbits, much much bigger, but the same colour white. Of course you can't touch them because they're very fierce and that's why they keep them behind a fence and there's water and they go in the water, but they can't get out to where the people are. They live in caves. Well, not really caves, but something shaped like caves, and that's where they live.

I liked the zoo better than the museum. I'm not saying I didn't like the museum, it's just that I liked the zoo better.

In the museum there are lots of things like statues that are called idols. The Indians made them a long time ago. And my mama told her friend Kay, because she was there too, she came to spend a few days here and then went back to the United States where she lives. Anyway, she told Kay she felt as if the idols could suddenly start moving, and they laughed, but I didn't feel that. And we also saw a huge huge wheel that was a calendar the Indians kept. That's what my mama and Kay said. And there are lots of other things too.

Later I asked my mama, what did you like best, the museum or the zoo? And she said both. But what did you like better, I kept asking her, because I wanted her to say the zoo, but she kept saying both. Not me.

Icon. Painted image representing the Virgin or the saints. The Virgin and the saints.

My mama says she doesn't believe in the Virgin, but I've never asked her if she believes in the saints.

I told her Marcela's papa and mama believe in her, and so do Señora Lena and Don Celso. Don Celso told me once that my mama doesn't believe in the Virgin because she's a gringo and gringos don't believe in the Virgin. I told my mama that and she said, partly. I didn't understand what she meant. But I asked her if I could believe in the Virgin, because I'm not a gringo, and she answered yes, if you want. So I believe in her.

Even though I hardly ever go to the parish church or any of the other churches where the Virgin is. Well, not her but her statue, but it's as if she was there.

I've only been to mass once, with Marcela and her papa and mama, one Sunday. And I saw her there.

Marcela's mama says the Virgin is the Mother of God and we need to believe that. My mama says God doesn't have a mother the way we have to have one.

But when I asked her how he was born then, she said she didn't know. And when I asked her if she believed in God, she said she didn't know that either. Afterwards I asked her, didn't she need to believe in all that?, and she said no.

I believe that God does exist, and the Virgin too, because I remember what Don Celso said.

When I went to mass with them that Sunday I saw people doing something and I didn't know what it was. Well, not everybody did it, but a lot of people did. Marcela's mama told me they were taking communion. And why aren't we taking communion?, I asked her. And she said she'd explain it to me later.

When the mass was over, she told me that only people who are not in a state of sin take communion. I didn't know what that meant so I asked her, but instead of answering me she didn't say a word and she kept looking and looking and looking at Marcela's papa. He finally said that a sin is an error people make, and when someone makes an error he has to talk to the priest about it and afterwards he can take communion. And I asked him when someone could talk to the priest about an error and he said, whenever we want. But I didn't really know what an error was, well, I sort of knew, because when a division doesn't come out right, for example, even though we say, I made a mistake, Señorita Estela says, let's try to find the error. And that's what I said to Marcela's papa, were those errors we should talk to the priest about?, and he said no, not those errors, another kind of error, and I asked him what kind and he said, when we commit errors that make other people suffer, your mama or your friends, that's what he said. And I told him that when I don't get good marks at school my mama suffers and he said that if we don't study hard, then that's an error we should talk to the priest about, and then I asked him why we didn't talk to the priest about our errors before mass so we could take communion, but he didn't answer me, he just smiled.

Later Marcela told me that she couldn't take communion because she still hasn't made her first communion, and that's the first time someone does what those people were doing that Sunday at mass. When are you going to make it?, I asked her and her mama said soon, very soon. Because I don't want to go to hell, said Marcela.

Do you think a place like that really exists, little horse? I had heard about hell before that Sunday. My mama and I talked about it once and she told me no, a place like that couldn't exist.

Don Celso and Señora Lena said it does exist and that's where the Devil lives. They said hell is nothing but flames and fire and that's where bad people go. When Señora Lena told me, it made me really scared because that was the first time someone told me that, and I even held on tight to her. But she told me not to worry, I wouldn't go to hell even if I died that very moment, that moment when she was telling me about it. Because you're an innocent child, she said. And I asked her, what if I die later?, and I kept staring at her and I was really scared and then she said no, no, no, not then either. That made me stop worrying.

That Sunday I said to Marcela, you and I won't go to hell because you're an innocent little girl and I'm an innocent little boy. And her papa said that's true. But Marcela asked him, and later on? Behave yourselves, he said, and nothing will happen to you.

So I'm going to behave myself every day, so I won't have to go to that house of flames. Because that's how it must be, a house that's always burning, with a fire that never ever ends.

Oh, little horse, now I feel even more afraid.

I'm going to write. I better write until my mama comes, so I don't have to feel more afraid, little horse.

# CHAPTER FIVE

# ESTEBAN

I am waiting for my mama who hasn't come home. It's very late at night and I'm scared because I just remembered about hell and other things. I haven't seen my mama since Friday afternoon when she told me she was going out and she'd see me later and I should go to bed early. Now it's Saturday. Saturday is almost over. A little while ago I went to look at the alarm clock and it was quarter past ten, but now it's even later. I know this even though I haven't gone back to look at the clock, the clock only stops when the spring winds down but even when the spring winds down it doesn't matter, it's going to get late even if the spring winds down on all the clocks in the world. Only if the sun stopped, and the moon and the earth and the stars and everything, then it wouldn't get later.

What I just read to you is what I wrote, little horse. I fell asleep after that because I was really sleepy. I didn't stay awake to wait for my mama. But it doesn't matter because she didn't come anyway. I went to look in her room and she wasn't there.

And don't think she came back and then went out again, no. Because her bed is still made. And besides it's barely seven o'clock and she only gets up at seven on weekdays when she goes to the Institute. Not on Sundays. And today is Sunday.

Where could she be? Now we have to go looking for her. First I'll eat breakfast, and if she doesn't arrive we'll go. I'll leave a note on the table telling her that I went out looking for her. Oh, if she came back now it would make me so happy.

I'd like to be big already and working so I could give my mama lots of money and she wouldn't have to work so hard. Then on Friday nights I'd have the right to have fun. But I wouldn't go out with anybody except my mama. I'd take her to a restaurant and we'd order some of everything, everything, and I'd order my orange pop and a huge dish of strawberry ice-cream and she'd get vanilla with chocolate sauce, her favourite.

Oh, we'd have a lot of fun together, a lot a lot a lot of fun. And you'd come with us too, because you're going to be with me all my life and we're going to keep on playing together even when I'm really really really old and if you don't play with me when I'm really old I'm going to feel very sad.

But don't think I'm serious when I say that. Because

I know what happens. I'm the one who has to go on playing with you. So I'll go on playing with you all my life all all all my life. Because I love you so much, little horse.

*

It's very early. It's not even eight-thirty yet. Well, on a weekday that isn't so early, because if the bells ring eight-thirty when I'm going by here it means I'm late. But on Sunday eight-thirty is early.

And not just for me, for lots of people. Because there's no one around. Well, hardly anyone. There's that man washing his car, and the boy and the man giving shoeshines in the corner of the square.

When I leave school and walk by here, I see lots of gringos sitting on the benches sunbathing. But not just gringos, Mexicans too. And there are ladies. Some people bring their dogs tied to little chains. It's almost three o'clock then, not early like it is now.

Look at those pigeons. There are always pigeons on that corner because the man who gives shoeshines, the one who's always walking around with his sombrero and his dark glasses, he gives them little bits of bread so the pigeons hang around him. Well, there are pigeons in other parts of the square too, wherever they can find food and wherever people throw them bread.

And the people on their way to mass. But they don't stay outside. We just see them walk by and go straight into the church.

You know something, little horse? I don't know where to look for my mama. La Fragua and Mama Mía are closed. There's nobody in the streets now. San Miguel is lonely at this hour. Unless she went over to the market. But why would she go to the market? To buy things. No, I don't think so. But anyway, should we see if we can find her there?

*

There's my school. But nobody's there now because it's closed, we're all somewhere else.

Once I came here on a Saturday morning with Marcela and her mama. They had agreed to meet Señora Green, because they were going to arrange the party for Mother's Day. The school was quiet, very very quiet. Marcela and I sat in the archway and we looked at the fountain and the bougainvillea around the patio and we didn't say a thing, as if we thought we weren't at the school but in someone's house. But it was the school.

It gave me a strange feeling, a bit sad, and I thought, some day I won't be coming to school, when I'm big, and that's what made me feel sad, I don't know why. Because when I'm big I'm going to work and my mama will spend more time with me, but that's not what I was thinking about then, instead I thought about the day I won't be going to my school any more.

Then we went into the classrooms and in one of them we found a sweater on one of the desks and a pencil thrown on the floor, and we left it there and we left the sweater where it was too.

That time we could hear our steps really loud, because we were the only ones walking around in the classrooms and the whole school was quiet quiet quiet, like asleep, and we weren't saying anything. Well, almost nothing, because Marcela said the sweater belonged to Fox.

Afterwards we went to the other courtyard, where the old tires are, but Marcela and I didn't talk about jumping off the wall because both of us are afraid to do it.

But I remembered Roberto, the one who jumps the most, and the other children who throw themselves off the wall and I could almost hear their cries. But not really, everything was all quiet and the silence felt so loud inside my ears.

If I didn't know what day it is today, just looking at the street where the school is would tell me it's Sunday.

Look, those are the stands against the church wall where they sell little cars and jack-knives and harmonicas and eyeglasses and everything, but those stands are always there. No, I would know it was Sunday because there are ladies selling avocados from their baskets on the sidewalks, and men selling herbs I don't know, and that stand with the sweaters and blankets hanging on the wall and others with copper trays and kettles, and the stand where they sell those huge loaves of bread they call Acámbaro bread. And there are lots of people buying and people are walking around in their clean clothes and some of the young women are coming from mass. I can tell because they have their shawls in their hands.

There are lots of stands here too. At the foot of the green statue. Can you imagine, little horse, if one day Don Ignacio Allende said to his horse, let's go!, and they jumped over all the stands and the houses and went flying flying flying all the way to the other side of the big dam and then went racing through the countryside up and down the hills, so happy not to be statues, to be alive again? Because doesn't the horse look like he's about to jump? But they already died, they died a long time ago, in the war. Well, not those two, but him and his horse.

There are lots of people but my mama isn't around here. I can't see her, no matter how hard I look. There are campesinos and ladies and a little girl with her papa eating carnitas in a roll and she's holding two Pepsis. I'd like to have a carnitas sandwich, with an orange pop. We haven't had carnitas for a long time, ever since that time it made my mama sick and she never bought it again.

There are lots of things for sale. Clothes, little pots like the ones they make in Dolores Hidalgo and strawberries and avocados and limes and metal griddles to cook tortillas and lots of things.

There's no sign, no sign at all of my mama, little horse. But let's go inside where they sell the fruit and see if we can find her. I don't think she's going to be there. If I don't find her I'm going to go to Virginia's house and see if she knows where she could be.

This is where they sell flowers and vegetables and fruit. They make chocolate milkshakes in this stand. Mmm, I'd love to have a huge one, but how can I pay for it? If my mama was here with me she wouldn't buy me one anyway, because she says the milk isn't pasteurized and it can make me sick. I believe it because that's what she said, but why doesn't it make all the people who drink chocolate milkshakes sick? Or maybe it does but I don't know them so I don't realize it.

She won't let me try the food they sell in these stands either, even though I love the smell of the frijoles and the chile.

Or the apples or the grapes or the peaches, because we have to wash the fruit first. But she lets me eat oranges in the street. The only thing I never feel like eating is moronga, blood sausage, because it looks like mud and smells awful.

No sign of her, little horse. I knew she wasn't going to be here, but I have to look for her everywhere. Now let's go to Virginia's house.

*

Virginia told me to go home and wait for her, that my mama will come home, that she hasn't seen her since Friday night when she was at La Fragua with some friends but afterwards she went home to her own house.

Virginia was still in bed, she didn't even open the door, she told me all that from the window.

I asked her who else might be able to tell me where she was and she said she had no idea and the best thing for me to do was go home and not worry, she'd be back, maybe she was there already.

But she wasn't. The house is still empty, just the way we left it this morning. She hasn't been here. I found my note under my cereal bowl.

That's why I came here to the park. But first I went to the Institute, to see if she was there. Because sometimes she goes there on Sunday, when the students sell the things they make, their paintings or their hand-weaving or their ceramics.

But there wasn't a single student in the courtyard. Nobody was there. Well, just a man who asked me what I was doing there and I told him I was looking for my mama.

And why are you looking for her here?, he asked me, and I told him, because she works at the Institute, and I told him her name.

Oh yes, yes I know her, I work here too, he said, but she hasn't been here today, nobody comes on Sundays. Except when they sell things, I said to him. Yes, he said.

Then I asked him if he was a friend of my mama's and he said no, I just know her by sight.

The man was sitting on a bench near a door and he had lots of keys in his hand, tied together on a string like mine, and he kept twirling and twirling them, like he was playing with them.

I asked him why he needed so many keys and he told me they were the keys to the classrooms.

ESTEBAN

Who's going to come to study today?, I asked him and he said nobody, but he carried the keys around, back and forth, that's what he said, back and forth, because he didn't have anything to do.

I told him I only had one key and I wore it on a string too, but I hung it around my neck, and that was my mama's idea so I wouldn't lose the key.

That's how you have to carry them, he said, on a little string so they don't get lost.

Then I asked him what he did there and he told me he swept and opened and closed the classrooms.

Even on Sunday?, I asked him and he said that on Sundays they didn't open the classrooms and there were a few people who did the same thing as him and even though it was Sunday they had to work and stand guard and they took turns. One Sunday it was one man's turn and the next Sunday another man's and so on, he said, because people come to visit the school and it has to be open and everything has to be clean.

After I told him it was time for me to go, I had to go on looking for my mama because I hadn't seen her since Friday, I told him, if she comes by here tell her I'm looking for her.

He told me he didn't think she'd be by, but if she comes I'll tell her, he said. And then he asked me why I didn't go looking for her at her friends' houses and I told him I'd already gone to Virginia's house. Virginia?, he asked and I said yes. Is she a gringo who works here too?, he asked me and I told him yes, and he said, I know her by sight too.

But she's not here in the park either. I walked all around it but she's not here. I'm tired from walking so much and that's why I sat down in front of the basketball nets.

It's really hot, the sun is hot and the boys and girls who are playing are sweating, their T-shirts are wet but they go on running and running.

I sat down to rest. I'm going to stay here a little bit longer and after I'll go back to the house and the square and the market and everywhere, if she still hasn't come home.

I think they must have opened La Fragua by now, and I'm going to ask there and at Mama Mía too.

Look at the herons. They live in the trees here in the park. I'd like to be able to fly around on a heron, from up there I could go looking everywhere everywhere.

Well, I could only see the streets, not inside the houses. Well, I could see into the patios of the houses. At least the houses that have patios, because mine doesn't have one. Or a garden like Marcela's house.

# CHAPTER SIX

I spent the whole day looking for my mama. I haven't seen her for two days, it seems like three because we say Friday, Saturday and Sunday. But no. From Friday to Saturday makes one, from Saturday to Sunday makes two.

And it doesn't make two whole days, because Sunday isn't over yet. But to me they've felt really really really long, like a thousand days.

I've been all around San Miguel and I still haven't found her. I went to the town square really early and to the market and to Virginia's house and to the Institute and the park and she wasn't in any of those places.

After I went to Mama Mía. She wasn't there either. All I saw was some children with a lady eating pizza. Then I went into La Fragua and I asked a man who was on his way out if he had seen my mama and he asked me, who is your mama?, and I said Emily. Emily?, he said and I repeated her name and said she worked at the Institute. I don't know her, he said, because a lot of people come here. Maybe she's inside, I said, and he said no, there's no one inside right now.

I haven't seen her since Friday when she left the house, I told him. And what about your papa?, he asked me. And I told him I don't know anything about him. About when he went out? No, I told him, I mean I don't know who he is, all I know is that he lives in the United States, but I've never seen him. We live alone, just the two of us, my mama and me, I told him.

Then the man messed up my hair and told me he had to go out right then, but I should go on looking for her and if I didn't find her I should come back and he would help me look for her.

He asked me how old I was and he called me kid. How old are you kid? I told him eight. Eight? Well, I'm going to be nine soon. I know I have around seven months to go before my birthday, but that's what I told him.

Then he told me to come back if I didn't find her and he went out and I didn't walk any farther inside, all I could see was an archway and a fountain in one corner and lots of potted plants and tables and chairs. And I didn't ask him his name, I don't know why I didn't think of it, but anyway he's easy to recognize because he's very tall and he has white hair.

After that I went to look for her at the market again

and I went walking up and down lots of streets but I didn't find her. I went back to La Fragua and I asked a boy who was hanging around there about that man and if he knew him. Yes, he said, he's the boss, I work here. He won't be back until night-time, he told me. And that was in the afternoon. That's why I decided to go sit in the square, and as soon as it started to get dark, I walked back to La Fragua again, but another man told me he wasn't there and I said, he must have come back because he's the boss and it's night-time and a boy told me he comes at night. He said yes, he does, but he arrives later.

Look, little horse, almost two pages, my hand even hurts a little because I wrote all that. Well, it doesn't hurt, let's say it feels really tired.

And then I didn't go back to the square, instead I came home. I was so tired and I was hungry. I'm going to eat something and then I'll go back there and ask the man to help me look for her.

\*

The man hasn't come yet. I'm going to sit here on the sidewalk and wait for him. I already went inside and asked two men if they know my mama and I told them her name, but they said no.

There are lots of people in there that I've never seen. The music is really loud. There are men playing guitars and one of them has lots of drums all around him and another one is playing an organ. I'm very tired and I feel really sleepy, little horse.

I've been everywhere. I even went to that place called El Patio even though I know she never goes there. I've heard her tell the men she doesn't like going to El Patio. She wasn't there.

I think I should go home to bed instead, because after all tomorrow is Monday and she has to go to work at the Institute, and she'll come home to sleep tonight so she can get up early tomorrow morning. I hope so.

# CHAPTER SEVEN

I fell asleep. Nobody woke me up in time, because my mama didn't come home. If Marcela's papa had come by at eight I'd be at school now.

When I heard somebody knocking it made me happy because I thought it was my mama, just like that, but then I said no, my mama must be asleep, besides she has her key, but what if she lost it? All right, so it must be Don Celso, but he delivers the milk in the afternoon, and I was all confused, was it afternoon, night-time, was it my mama, Don Celso, and I didn't think it was Monday already.

And they kept knocking and knocking and knocking and then I got up and went to open the door. It was Marcela's papa and that really surprised me. The sun was shining in the street and I looked at the clock from the door and I saw that it was eleven o'clock in the morning, and I also saw my mama's bed, still made, the way it had been since Friday morning.

Then Marcela's papa said, Esteban, and I said hi. Then he walked by me and went to sit on my mama's bed and he stared and stared and stared at me, as if he was really worried about something. And I thought it was because I hadn't gone to school and that he and Marcela's mama and Marcela thought something bad had happened to me, and that's why he had come looking for me.

So I told him that I didn't go to school because my mama wasn't home and I didn't wake up on time. That I had gone looking for her everywhere and couldn't find her. I haven't seen her since Friday, I told him.

But he went on looking at me, sort of sad, and I didn't know why. And then he asked me if I had my grandma's address and I said no.

Do you know where your mama keeps the letters she receives?, he asked me and I told him, over there beside her books. And he went and looked for them.

When he found them he started reading them one after another. But he didn't finish them, he just read a bit of one, a bit of another.

Then he finally found something in one of the letters and he said, here it is, and he picked up the envelope and read the back of it, and repeated, yes, here it is.

Is it my grandma's address?, I asked him and he said yes. What for?, I asked him, but he said, take some clothes and anything else you want, because I'm going to take you home with me.

Then he started to gather up the letters and put them back beside the dictionaries.

Why?, I asked him and he just told me to do what he said.

All right, I told him, but before we go to your house you have to take me to the Institute so I can let my mama know.

Go get your clothes, he said, and I obeyed him.

We still haven't been to the Institute. I guess I'm going to leave my clothes at his house first, along with my things for school, because he told me to bring them with me too, and then we'll go to see my mama.

But I don't know why he wanted to do it this way. My house is closer to the Institute. El Atascadero is much farther.

When we arrived here Marcela's mama held me tight for a long time and kept crying the whole time. I heard him tell her that he had already sent the telegram, and I remembered that he stopped the car outside the telegraph office and went inside and I sat in the car waiting for him. Marcela isn't at home, she must be at school.

I don't know what's happening. All I know is Marcela's mama keeps looking at me and crying and he keeps telling her to calm down. I think something bad happened to him too, because today he's not smiling.

Take me to see my mama at the Institute, I say to him.

You can't see your mother any more, Esteban.

*

Marcela has been telling me not to cry all afternoon, but I can't stop doing it. Ever since her papa told me I won't be able to see my mama any more.

Don't cry Esteban, don't cry, she tells me, and she's crying too.

I remember that time my mama kept telling me the same thing, except she wasn't crying like Marcela is now, when the lady gave me the injection and she promised me a little present so I'd be quiet. Then I stopped. But now I can't stop, even though I'm crying without making much noise, and I keep hugging the present she gave me.

When I asked Marcela's papa where it happened, he just told me to try to calm down, because I was already crying. But I had asked him something and he wasn't answering me, so I kept asking him to tell me where, and he told me that later on he would tell me everything but not now, that I should do everything I could to calm down. But I couldn't and I kept crying and crying and crying. Louder than now.

And Marcela was the one who told me, but only a part of it, because she doesn't know everything either.

While she was telling me about it I stopped crying a bit, but after she told me I couldn't help myself and Marcela's mama even came to see what was happening.

She told me that her papa and her mama were

talking and they thought the two of us were still here in her bedroom upstairs, because when they saw Marcela her mama stopped talking and asked her if she'd heard and Marcela said yes and then her mama told her not to go and tell me. But Marcela didn't promise anything, so she could tell me that her mama was crying and said to her father that it had been a horrible, monstrous crime and she didn't understand how people like that could exist and that my mama had been tortured in such a cruel way and now what would become of me. And then her papa said he'd ask my grandma to let me live here with them, and if she said no he would insist that she leave me here at least until the end of the next school year.

Then Marcela said her father picked up a newspaper that was on the sofa and burned it in the fireplace, and he said, so neither one of them sees it.

How could anybody do something like that?, that's what Marcela said her mama was saying over and over again, when she saw her and stopped talking and told her not to go and tell me.

And I was crying very loud and Marcela's mama hugged me and told me now, now Esteban, don't cry now, and she was crying too.

After I heard him ask, what happened?, from the door of the bedroom, and she answered, Marcela told him, and then Marcela started crying and her papa told her, don't cry, little girl, don't cry, come here. And I felt the three of them hugging me.

Then her mama went to get a book of photographs

and she told us she was going to stay here with us to look at the book and read it, because there are words under the photographs.

It's a book with pictures of trees. There are forests. And Marcela's mama read about where there are red trees and I listened to her voice that was saying, in the autumn the woods, but it sounded far away, because I was thinking about the word crime and the word horrible and the word monstrous and the word tortured and the word cruel. And I wanted to know who had done it so I could kill him, the way he killed my mama.

And I remembered one of them who was yelling at her once in the middle of the night and I woke up and I went to see and they were both mad, because my mama was yelling too, but his yelling was louder.

He was yelling what about Vietnam, and what about Vietnam, remember that, remember that, he kept saying.

And my mama was yelling from the kitchen, that has nothing to do with me, but she said that to him in English and then he shouted, learn to speak Spanish if you want to live in Mexico, and he threw the glass he was holding in his hand and it broke on the floor. Then he left and slammed the door with a bang.

When I walked towards the kitchen I tried not to step on the glass so I wouldn't cut myself because I was barefoot, but I stepped on a piece and I started to bleed.

My mama came out of the kitchen and saw me and said, Esteban, that idiot woke you up, that's what she said, and I told her I'd cut myself and she gave me a hug.

Why was he yelling, mama?, I asked her and she said, he's drunk.

What is Vietnam?, I asked her, and she said, a country very far away. But it has nothing to do with you, I said to her without knowing what they were talking about. And she said, nothing Esteban, absolutely nothing to do with me.

Then she carried me to my bed and cleaned the blood off my foot with a cotton ball, and my cut really burned because she put alcohol on the cotton ball. So you don't get an infection, she said.

I never saw him again. Could it be him? Because he was yelling at her so mad. But that was a long time ago. And my mama had nothing to do with that Vietnam business. Anyway, if I knew where he lives I'd go looking for him with the police, so he could say if he was the one or not.

Stop crying now, Esteban, Marcela says to me from the floor where the book is still open, exactly where her mama left it when she went to the kitchen because she said it was time to eat and she'd call us soon.

I'm in Marcela's bed hugging my little horse, and I can't stop crying. I'm not hungry, I just feel very sad very sad very sad.

# Chapter Eight

Tomorrow my grandma is going back to the United States. I would've liked to take her all around San Miguel so she can see what it's like. But she doesn't feel like doing it now, and neither do I. Maybe next year, if she comes to get me or just to visit me, if she lets me live for ever with Marcela and her papa and her mama.

She said she didn't know what to do, I'm her grandson and she really loves me but she's very old and she's all alone and she doesn't feel capable of taking care of me.

I haven't heard anything about the father for years, she said, so for me it's as if he never existed. And since Marcela's mama doesn't speak English and my grandma doesn't speak Spanish, her papa and I told her what she was saying.

I told my grandma that I didn't want to leave, I don't want to, grandma, because this is where my mama is and I'm always going to stay close to her. And Marcela's mama asked what I was saying and he translated for her.

But my grandma said, I don't know, I don't know. I'll make my decision and next year I'll come to get you or at least visit you. And Marcela's papa said it in Spanish and her mama said yes, of course.

I hope she'll leave me. If she doesn't, when I'm big I'll come back to San Miguel anyway and I'll never leave here again.

My grandma came to see my mama's funeral. I didn't see my mama, I told them to let me, I told them to open the box, but Marcela's papa hugged me and told me it was better for me not to see her, better to remember her the way she used to be. So I couldn't see anything but the black box my mama was going in.

And I screamed really loud when the men were lowering her into the ground. Then they put bricks and cement on, like when they make houses, and then they covered her with earth. My grandma was crying hard too, and Virginia and other ladies I had never seen before, and Señorita Estela and Señora Green. And everyone from my school was there, but I didn't see if the boys and girls and the other teachers were crying. And when we came home, my mama stayed over there, beneath the earth and a lot of flowers.

*

We've turned off the light. I think Marcela has fallen asleep, because she's not talking any more. But I can't sleep. I can't stop thinking about my mama, about her face smiling in her passport picture, it's the only one I have. And I'm holding it tight under the covers, along with the little horse she gave me. I can hear the words of Marcela's papa, no Esteban, it's better for you to remember her the way she used to be.

My mama. Why did she die? Why are there crimes? Who killed her?

Hell does exist, mama, a place like that does exist, and the person who did it is going to go there when he dies.

I'm not at all sleepy, little horse, not at all. I wish I could sleep and dream about my mama, I wish the night would last a long long time, that it would never end so my mama and I could go everywhere together, very happy, just the two of us.

You know what, little horse? I can't grow up to work harder than her, the way I wanted. We would have had a lot of fun together on Friday nights. And I would have taken her to the sea too, to Puerto Angel and anywhere else she wanted to go. But I can't do it, little horse, I can't do it because there are crimes and they committed one with my mama.

I can't stop crying, I can't. Even when I'm thinking of things and I'm talking, there's something sort of stuck to my eyes and I'm sure it's never going to go away.

When they were putting the bricks and the cement and the earth on top.

Do you remember how scared I was in the house that night, when we were waiting for her? And how I kept asking myself why I was so scared and I said it was as if I'd had a nightmare? But even though I fell asleep I didn't have one, and I couldn't explain why I was so scared.

I think I did have one, but I didn't know it. Well, I didn't have one. But do you remember that Señorita Estela says we dream every night and we don't always remember our dreams? So it was something like that, as if I had been dreaming something really awful, that awful thing that happened to my mama, and at the same time I couldn't remember it, and all that was left was the fear of something I couldn't explain.